TOWER HAMLETS PUBLIC LIBRARY

D1324210

ESCAPE FROM THE
POP-UP PRISON

BY MICHAEL DAHL
ILLUSTRATED BY BRADFORD KENDALL

Librarian Reviewer
Laurie K. Holland
Media Specialist

Reading Consultant
Elizabeth Stedem
Educator/Consultant

Raintree is an imprint of Capstone Global Library Limited, a
company incorporated in England and Wales having its registered
office at 7 Pilgrim Street, London, EC4V 6LB – Registered
company number: 6695582

"Raintree" is a registered trademark of Pearson Education
Limited, under licence to Capstone Global Library Limited

Text © Stone Arch Books, 2009
First published by Stone Arch Books in 2008
First published in hardback in the United Kingdom in 2009
Firs~~~~~~~~~~~~~~~~~~~~~~~~~~~~~~~~~~~~2010

LONDON BOROUGH
TOWER HAMLETS

910 000 00237323	
HJ	26-Nov-2010
	£4.99
THCUB	

All rig~~~~~~~~~~~~~~~~~~~~~~~~~~~~~~~~~~~~~~duced
in any~~~~~~~~~~~~~~~~~~~~~~~~~~~~~~~~~~~ring it
in any~~~~~~~~~~~~~~~~~~~~~~~~~~~~~~~~~~~siently
or inc~~~~~~~~~~~~~~~~~~~~~~~~~~~~~~~~~~ut the
writte~~~~~~~~~~~~~~~~~~~~~~~~~~~~~~~~~~dance
with ~~~~~~~~~~~~~~~~~~~~~~~~~~~~~~~~~s Act
198~~~~~~~~~~~~~~~~~~~~~~~~~~~~~~~~~~ight
Lic~~~~~~~~~~~~~~~~~~~~~~~~~~~~~~~~~~ndon
EC1N~~~~~~~~~~~~~~~~~~~~~~~~~~~~~~~~owner's
w~~~~~~~~~~~~~~~~~~~~~~~~~~~~~~~~~~er.

Creative Director: Heather Kinseth
Senior Designer for Cover and Interior: Kay Fraser
Graphic Designer: Brann Garvey
Edited in the UK by Laura Knowles
Printed and bound in China by Leo Paper Products Ltd

ISBN 978-1406212754 (hardback)
13 12 11 10 09
10 9 8 7 6 5 4 3 2 1

ISBN 978-1406212617 (paperback)
14 13 12 11 10
10 9 8 7 6 5 4 3 2

British Library Cataloguing in Publication Data
Dahl, Michael.
Escape from the pop-up prison. -- (Library of doom)
813.5'4-dc22
A full catalogue record for this book is available
from the British Library.

TABLE OF CONTENTS

The Library of Doom is the world's largest collection of strange and dangerous books. The Librarian's duty is to keep the books from falling into the hands of those who would use them for evil purposes.

4

CHAPTER 1

THE MIDNIGHT STRANGERS

A girl **wakes** up at midnight.

She hears strange voices coming from <u>downstairs.</u>

She **creeps** out of her room to see who it is.

Strange men are talking to her father.

"You know the only way inside the Library," one of the men says. "Take us there, or else."

Who are they? the girl wonders.

The men **force** her father out
of the house.

From a safe distance, the girl
follows them.

She hides in the **shadows.**

The men walk through dozens of
dark streets and **alleys.**

CHAPTER 2

THE WAY IN

In a rundown part of town, the men stop in a small alley.

The girl's father points to an old poster on the wall. "That is the way in," he says.

"**Show us,**" says one of the men.

The girl's father pushes against one of the letters.

A `secret passageway` appears.

"Follow me," the girl's father says.

The men all slip through the entrance.

Now the girl knows where her father is taking the men.

They are **entering** a secret
hallway that leads to the
Library of Doom.

CHAPTER 3

THE PAPER TRAIL

The girl's father had once worked in the Library of Doom.

He had been a **page,** an assistant to the mysterious Librarian.

The girl knows that the Librarian and her father had been good friends.

Now, as the girl follows the
men, she sees the passage end at a
huge pit.

"We need to get to the other side!"
exclaims one of the men. "There is no
way across. Is this a **trick?**"

"It is not a trick," says the girl's father.

He pulls a book from his shirt pocket.

Then he **throws** the book into the pit.

The book flies open. Its pages **scatter** through the air.

Then the pages form themselves into a **long bridge.**

"This is the only way across," says the girl's father.

CHAPTER 4

THE POP-UP PRISON

On the other side of the vast pit is a huge, **stone platform.**

In the middle of the platform sits a **single book.**

"There it is!" shouts one of the men. "That's what we've come for."

The strangers **open** the book.

As they turn a page, a `prison` `cell` pops up out of the book.

There is a man trapped inside
the cell.

"At last!" he cries.

The strangers free the man.

Then they turn more pages.

On each page, another cell pops up with another prisoner inside.

The strangers **release** each prisoner.

The girl watches fearfully from the shadows.

"It is the Pop-up Prison," she says to herself. "The world's **deadliest criminals** were trapped in its pages."

What will happen now that they are **free?**

CHAPTER 5

FREE!

A bright light **flashes** from the huge pit.

It is the Librarian.

"What have you done?" he cries.

One of the strangers **shakes** his fist at the Librarian.

"Too late, Librarian," he shouts. "We have freed our friends."

"You will never be able to defeat all of us," the other man yells. "We are **too strong** for you."

The girl **runs** to her father.

"How could you do this?" she asks. "Why did you **betray** the Librarian?"

"Your father warned me," the Librarian tells her. "As soon as he pressed that poster, a **signal** told me he was here."

"So what?" says one of the prisoners. "We are free. Now we can **rule the world!**"

The Librarian smiles.

"You are not in the world. You are in the **Library of Doom,**" he says. "And here, I rule."

The father pulls his daughter to the paper bridge.

As they run across the bridge, the pages **fall away** behind them.

The criminals **yell** and **scream** from the stone platform.

"Don't worry," the father tells the girl. "As I said, this was the only way in."

"And your father **never lies**," says the Librarian.

Then the Librarian adds, "My pages can always be trusted."

THE END

A PAGE FROM THE LIBRARY OF DOOM

MORE ABOUT POP-UP AND MOVABLE BOOKS

Pop-up books have been around for hundreds of years. They were originally known as "movable books" since objects and sections in them moved.

The first movable books were printed for adults, not children. One of the earliest movables, printed in Switzerland in 1543, was a book on anatomy. It showed the inside of a human body in different layers.

Dean & Son, a publisher in Great Britain in the 1800s, made the first pop-up books designed specifically for children. The books contained a special ribbon with each page. When the ribbon was pulled, the page would open up into a 3-dimensional display.

The person who designs the pop-ups for a book is called a **paper engineer**.

Today's pop-up books are all made by hand. Most of them are assembled in Central America or Singapore.

It may take as many as 60 people to put together one pop-up book.

Modern pop-up books have been made that contain electric lights and recorded music.

Robert Sabuda and Matthew Reinhart are wizards of modern pop-up books. They are famous for their pop-ups on prehistoric creatures. Some of their books use more than one hundred pieces of paper to help create the 3-D effects.

ABOUT THE AUTHOR

Michael Dahl is the author of more than 100 books for children and young adults. He has twice won the AEP Distinguished Achievement Award for his non-fiction. His Finnegan Zwake mystery series was chosen by the Agatha Awards to be among the five best mystery books for children in 2002 and 2003. He collects books on poison and graveyards, and lives in a haunted house in Minneapolis, USA.

ABOUT THE ILLUSTRATOR

Bradford Kendall has enjoyed drawing for as long as he can remember. As a boy, he loved to read comic books and watch old monster films. He graduated from the Rhode Island School of Design with a BFA in Illustration. He has owned his own commercial art business since 1983, and lives in Providence, Rhode Island, USA, with his wife, Leigh, and their two children Lily and Stephen. They also have a cat named Hansel and a dog named Gretel.

GLOSSARY

assistant (ah-SIS-tuhnt) – a person who helps somebody else

betray (bi-TRAY) – to reveal a secret and break someone's trust

mysterious (miss-TIHR-ee-uhs) – hard to explain or understand

page (PAYJ) – a young servant or assistant

passageway (PASS-ij-way) – a secret tunnel that people use to pass from one place to another

platform (PLAT-form) – a flat surface that is high off the ground

rundown (RUHN-doun) – old and needing repairs

signal (SIG-nuhl) – something done to communicate a warning, such as a noise or movement

vast (VAST) – very large in size

DISCUSSION QUESTIONS

1. Do you think it was safe for the girl to follow her father and the strange men? What would you have done?

2. The girl's father was forced to reveal the secret location of the Library of Doom. Is it okay to share some secrets with others? Why or why not?

3. If you could be trapped inside of a book, what book would you choose? Explain your answer.

WRITING PROMPTS

1. In this book, the author didn't reveal too much information about the girl. That's part of what makes the story mysterious. Use your imagination and write more about this character.

2. Pretend you are one of the criminals trapped on the stone platform. Describe how you would escape from the Library of Doom.

3. Family members make great characters for a book. Write about one or more of your family members.

MORE BOOKS TO READ

This story may be over, but there are many more dangerous adventures in store for the Librarian. Will the Librarian be able to escape the cave of the deadly giant bookworms? Will he defeat the rampaging Word Eater in time to save the world? You can only find out by reading the other books from the Library of Doom...